THE WILD SMURF

A SMURFS GRAPHIC NOVEL BY Peyo

WITH THE COLLABORATION OF
LUC PARTHOENS AND THIERRY CULLIFORD — SCRIPT
ALAIN MAURY AND LUC PARTHOENS — ARTWORK
NINE — COLOR

PAPERCUTZ™
NEW YORK

SMURFS GRAPHIC NOVELS AVAILABLE FROM PAPERCUTZ ™

1. THE PURPLE SMURFS
2. THE SMURFS AND THE MAGIC FLUTE
3. THE SMURF KING
4. THE SMURFETTE
5. THE SMURFS AND THE EGG
6. THE SMURFS AND THE HOWLIBIRD
7. THE ASTROSMURF
8. THE SMURF APPRENTICE
9. GARGAMEL AND THE SMURFS
10. THE RETURN OF THE SMURFETTE
11. THE SMURF OLYMPICS
12. SMURF VS. SMURF
13. SMURF SOUP
14. THE BABY SMURF
15. THE SMURFLINGS
16. THE AEROSMURF
17. THE STRANGE AWAKENING
    OF LAZY SMURF
18. THE FINANCE SMURF
19. THE JEWEL SMURFER
20. DOCTOR SMURF
21. THE WILD SMURF

- THE SMURF CHRISTMAS
- FOREVER SMURFETTE
- SMURFS MONSTERS

THE SMURFS graphic novels are available in paperback for $5.99 each and in hardcover for $10.99 each, except for THE SMURFS #21, which is $7.99 in paperback and $12.99 in hardcover, at booksellers everywhere. You can also order online at papercutz.com. Or call 1-800-886-1223, Monday through Friday, 9 – 5 EST. MC, Visa, and AmEx accepted. To order by mail, please add $4.00 for postage and handling for first book ordered, $1.00 for each additional book and make check payable to NBM Publishing. Send to: Papercutz, 160 Broadway, Suite 700, East Wing, New York, NY 10038.

THE SMURFS graphic novels are also available digitally wherever e-books are sold.

PAPERCUTZ.COM

THE WILD SMURF

© Peyo - 2016 - Licensed through Lafig Belgium - www.smurf.com

English translation copyright © 2016 by Papercutz.
All rights reserved.

"The Wild Smurf"
BY PEYO
WITH THE COLLABORATION OF
LUC PARTHOENS AND THIERRY CULLIFORD FOR THE SCRIPT,
ALAIN MAURY AND LUC PARTHOENS FOR ARTWORK,
NINE FOR COLORS.

"School for Fairies"
BY PEYO

Joe Johnson, SMURFLATIONS
Adam Grano, SMURFIC DESIGN
Janice Chiang, LETTERING SMURFETTE
Matt. Murray, SMURF CONSULTANT
Brittanie Black, SMURF COORDINATOR
Jeff Whitman, ASSISTANT MANAGING SMURF
Jim Salicrup, SMURF-IN-CHIEF

PAPERBACK EDITION ISBN: 978-1-62991-575-3
HARDCOVER EDITION ISBN: 978-1-62991-576-0

PRINTED IN CHINA SEPTEMBER 2016 BY WKT CO. LTD.
3/F PHASE 1 LEADER INDUSTRIAL CENTRE
188 TEXACO ROAD, TSEUN WAN, N.T., HONG KONG

Papercutz books may be purchased for business or promotional use. For information on bulk purchases please contact Macmillan Corporate and Premium Sales Department at (800) 221-7945 x5442.

DISTRIBUTED BY MACMILLAN
FIRST PAPERCUTZ PRINTING

THE WILD SMURF

Peyo

THE WILD SMURF

It's summer's end, and it's hot in the Land of the Smurfs... Very hot!

It's so hot in the village that nothing is astir. Well, almost...

My glass of sarsaparilla juice is empty! So smurf me another one!

I see not everyone's suffering too much from the heat wave, Jokey Smurf! What could Brainy Smurf have done to deserve such punishment?

Hee hee! I bet him he couldn't smurf for an hour without saying: "And as Papa Smurf always says..."

Of course, he lost! And now, even an earthquake couldn't smurf me from my place!

RUMMBLE

1

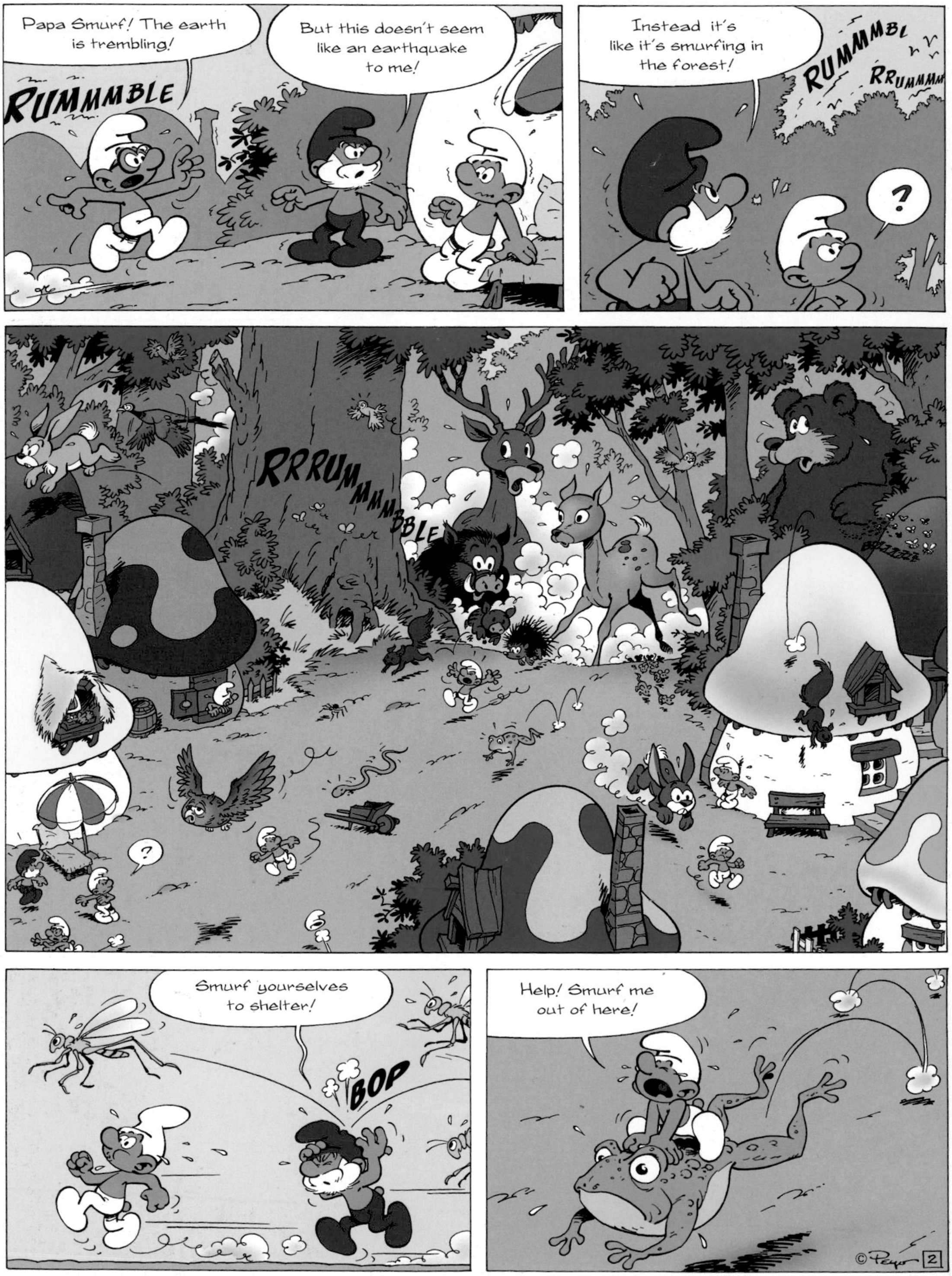
Papa Smurf! The earth is trembling!
RUMMMBLE
But this doesn't seem like an earthquake to me!
Instead it's like it's smurfing in the forest!
RUMMMBL
RRUMMMM
?
RRRUMMMMBLE
?
Smurf yourselves to shelter!
BOP
Help! Smurf me out of here!
© Peyo 2

But I told you I didn't do anything. Leave me alone!

⸮Whew⸮ **SAFE!**

SLAM

CRASH

⸮Pft!⸮ What a crash!

Luckily our houses are solidly smurfed!

Hey! My laundry!

Okay! I think we can smurf out! They're leaving!

Well, I never! What's smurfed into them?

?!

There's the answer to your question, Jokey Smurf! The forest is on fire!

3

DING DONG DING

FIRE! FIRE!

DING DONG

Go smurf some buckets! Smurf a chain from the river! Dig some trenches! Quick! The fire is upon us!

Come on, smurf on the flames with branches!

What about the chain? Why isn't it smurfing? The water isn't coming!

And hup! And hup!

?

Dopey Smurf, we told you to smurf some buckets, not colanders!

Really?

EEEEEE! My house is on fire!

Mine, too!

4

It's no use! The fire is spreading! I no longer have a choice if I want to smurf the village!

I'll smurf what I need in my laboratory!

Hefty Smurf! Grouchy Smurf! Come with me!

But what about the fire, Papa Smurf? Where are we going?

To the dam!

A few moments later, at the dam...

Go ahead, Grouchy Smurf! Smurf it between the two poles there!

Very gently!

That's fine! Now smurf the fuse!

Done? Then climb up quick!

gssssssssss

And what do we do now, Papa Smurf?

...Now?

sssssssssss

Run for your smurfs! It's going to blow up!

Me, I don't like **BLAM**s!

BLAM

5

In a few seconds, an enormous mass of water rushes towards the village...

What's going on?! Is that water we asked for coming?

...washes over everything in its path...

It's coming! It's coming!

?

...and soon puts out the fire.

SSSSSS

SSSSSS

PLOOOF

Later...

My little Smurfs! You're safe and smurf!

SPLISH

SPLISH

SPLISH

Yes, Papa Smurf! But the village is completely smurfed!

Don't worry about that, we'll quickly resmurf it! So long as everyone is here! By the way has anyone seen Brainy Smurf?

6

Smurf me out of here or else I'll tell Papa Smurf!

Sometime later...

⌐Pff.¬ We have to resmurf practically the whole village! A real smurficult job! Luckily, Papa Smurf is smurfing on the bright side of things!

But when I saw him, he seemed preoccupied.

Look! There he is in the middle of a conversation with Farmer Smurf!

I wonder what they could be smurfing about?

And you're saying the whole harvest is lost?!

Yes! Everything the fire didn't smurf, the water has spoiled!

Hmmm! It's worse than I feared! Our supplies are almost oxomurfed!

And the forest around the village has been destroyed so there's no question of harvesting anything! Something must be done! I'll talk to the Smurf's tomorrow!

And the next day...

Dear Smurfs! The situation is grave! We're almost out of food, and the winter is at hand! If we don't smurf some new supplies, we'll suffer from hunger again!*

OH!

OH! OOH!

Me, I don't like being hungry!

⌐Crunch!¬ For once, I agree with you!

Shhh!

That's why I've decided we'll go smurf food in the northern part of the forest because it wasn't smurfed by the fire!

Begin the preparations and smurf up early! We'll leave tomorrow morning!

The northern part of the forest!? ⌐Gulp!¬ It seems there are lots of weird smurfs there!

Really?

:See "The Hungry Smurfs," from THE SMURFS #4 "The Smurfette," of course!

Early in the morn...

Hurry up, Lazy Smurf! We're late!

ZZZZ

All right, now that everyone is here, we can smurf!

And the caravan of Smurfs sets out through a tortured landscape...

Despite the cold nights...

Sickly Smurf, I'll tell Papa Smurf you're smurfing all the covers!

CHITTER CHATTER

Despite the dangers of the trip...

Give me your hand, Brainy Smurf!

The Smurfs soon reach their journey's goal...

↯Brr!↯ This forest isn't like at our home! It gives me goosesmurf!

I told you it was a weird forest! It must be full of horrible monsters ready to smurf us alive!

↯Gulp!↯

?

Ha! Ha! Ha! Listen to all the sillismurf! He tells himself smurfs and he gets scared over nothing!

8

Ahhh! What's that?

Getting afraid over nothing, eh?

Halt! We're here! Smurf yourself into several groups and start gathering food!

Without delay, the Smurfs set to work...

Hey, you! Don't go too far away!

No, no, Papa Smurf!

Mmm! I love blueberries! I just can't resist... I'll smurf one of them!

?

What's that? Something moved behind me?!

CRAC

Uh... Is someone there? Is that you, Jokey Smurf?

Heh, heh! I'm sure it's you! ¿Gulp!¿ You won't be able to smurf me a fright!

What a strange feeling! It's as though someone is watching me!

It's a smurfily disagreeable sensation!

Uh... Sorry, Brainy Smurf!

SHPLUTZ

I'll tell Papa Smurf!

This forest doesn't seem right to me. What's more, you can't hear a single noise!

That's true, Papa Smurf! We should smurf back to the village now that our baskets are full!

Come, come! Don't worry! It's just your imagination smurfing tricks on you!

OOOEEOOOEEOoo!

I think it would be better not to smurf here too long, after all! Gather everyone! We're leaving!

What was it, Papa Smurf?

Hurry up, Greedy Smurf, we're returning to the village! You definitely don't want to get yourself smurfed by monsters!

Monsters or not, I'm certainly not going to leave behind all these good hazelnuts!

OOPS!

10

A hazelnut is a hazelnut!

GRRRR!

?!

Uh... A... After all, hazelnuts smurf me stomach aches!

ZOOM

GRRR!

Hey! Wait! Don't smurf without me...

Later, far away, in the Land of the Smurfs...

Curses! All my traps are empty!

That blasted fire didn't only destroy part of the forest, it also chased away all the game!

Hey, that's weird, I don't recognize this place!

We didn't come this way earlier! I wonder what part of the forest we're in?!

?

?!

11

15

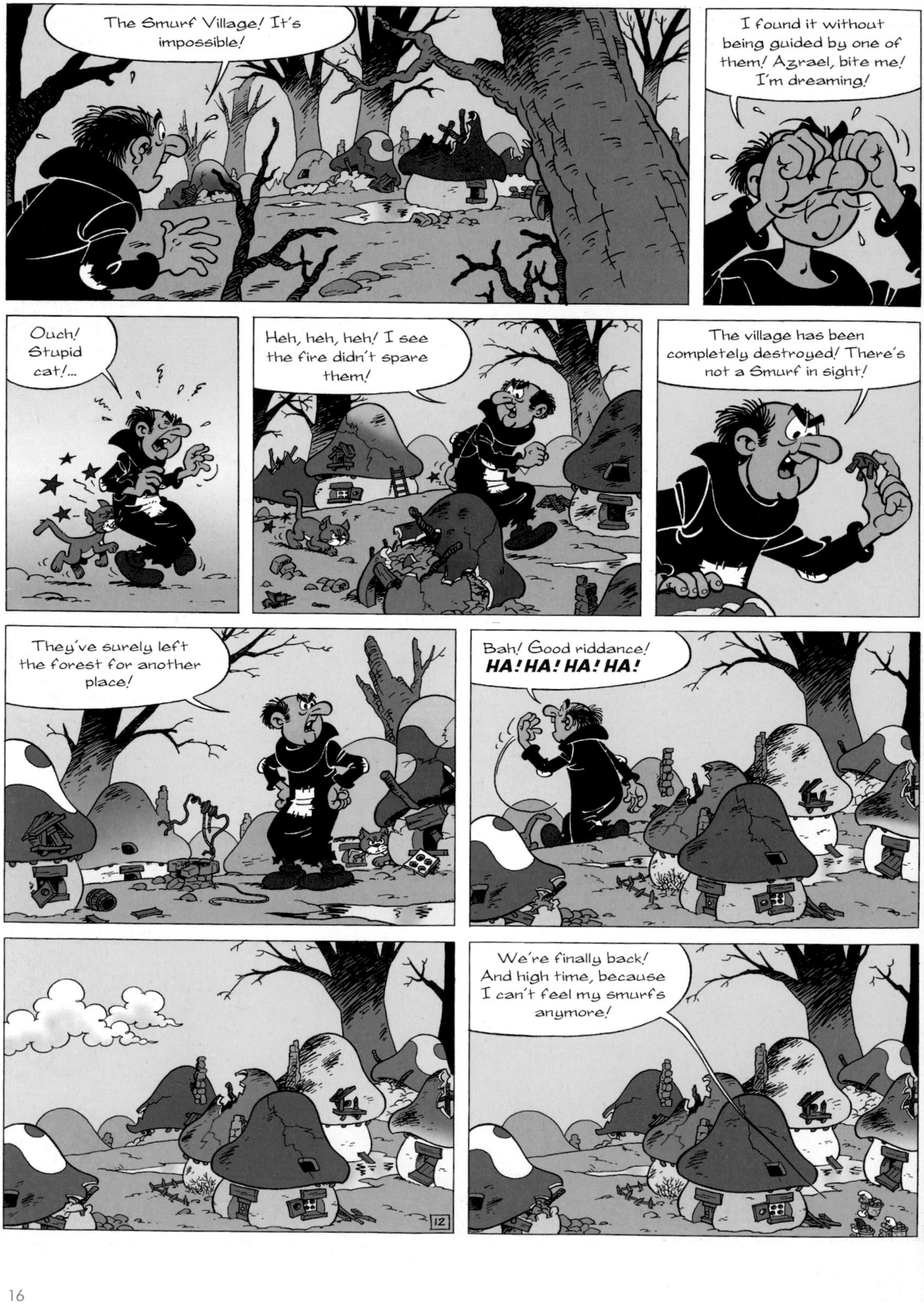

The Smurf Village! It's impossible!
I found it without being guided by one of them! Azrael, bite me! I'm dreaming!
Ouch! Stupid cat!...
Heh, heh, heh! I see the fire didn't spare them!
The village has been completely destroyed! There's not a Smurf in sight!
They've surely left the forest for another place!
Bah! Good riddance! HA! HA! HA! HA!
12
We're finally back! And high time, because I can't feel my smurfs anymore!

Papa Smurf! Look!

Footprints!

Hmm! It seems that, after the forest fire, it's possible to smurf the way to the village! We'll have to be more careful!

Let's go, my little Smurfs! Take heart! We're going to resmurf our village, and it'll be even smurfier than before!

Later, while the reconstruction of the village is in full swing...

PLOF

YIPPEE! It's winter!

Aren't you coming to smurf in the snow, Grouchy Smurf?

Me, I don't like snow!

Every time I go smurf in the snow with them, something happens to me! So, I'll smurf off by myself!

CRRRRR

?

WUMMP

Me, I don't like WUMMPs!

Unfortunately, that peaceful calm doesn't last. One morning...

Papa Smurf! Papa Smurf!

I assure you, Papa Smurf! Someone smurfed a bag of hazelnuts last night from the supplies!

Are you sure?

13

You see! He even smurfed footprints while going in and coming out of the supply room!

You're right!

?

I'm sure it was Greedy Smurf!

Hey! That's not even true!

It's a fact that these prints smurfily resemble those of a Smurf, but barefoot! That's strange in the winter!...

Okay! Handy Smurf! Smurf me one of your old locks!

Right away, Papa Smurf!

BRRRP

There! I don't like doing this, but we can't let someone smurf our meager provisions from us!

CLIC CLAC

And also, that'll allow us to smurf to Poet Smurf's new romantic poems tonight, in peace and calm!... Don't forget! Everybody be there!

This doesn't sound so good.

⸱Pfft!⸱ Right! His romantic writings are always so smurfing!

No way! I was talking about the footprints!

Oh? Uh... Yes... Of course!...

14

That night, at the theater, everyone's talking...

And a whole bag of hazelnuts was smurfed!

Really?!

No!

There were even Smurfprints in the snow!

Unbelievable!

Shh! It's starting!

Smurfprints? But then it is one of us!

For Smurf's sake! That's right! I hadn't smurfed of that!

Well, smurf! Who could it be?

In any case if it was barefoot prints, it can't be Sickly Smurf!

Obviously! But I know who it is! Like I said earlier, I'm sure it was Greedy Smurf who smurfed that sack!

And what's more, like Papa Smurf always says--

?!

RAP RAP RAP

Excuse me, Smurfs! Maybe you could let your friend Poet Smurf smurf his poems to us!

A few poems later...

Poet Smurf smurfily knows how to play with words!

Yum!... Especially when he smurfs about fruits in a soliloquy!... Yum!... It was smurfily appetizing!

Hey, speaking of which, I'll smurf by the supply room, just to take a look!

OH!

© Peyo

15

19

Look! Someone has smurfed the lock and has entered the supply room again!

?

?

Maybe the thief's still there! Let's try to smurf him!

?!

?!

But... Hey! If all the Smurfs were at the theater tonight, it wasn't one of us! ⸲Gulp!⸲

He's right, Handy Smurf! Let's... Let's go smurf Papa Smurf instead!

Shh! Follow me!

Do you smurf anything?

?

Aaah! There! On the beam! The thing... Its... Its eyes! Like back there!

GRRRRR!

Hup!

GRRRR!

!

OOF!

16

Hey! He's running away! **STOP, THIEF!** Smurf him!

Wait! I'm Handy Smurf! He won't escape me.

POW

HA! HA! HA!

Hup!

Handy Smurf! What smurfed?

The thief has smurfed into the supply room again! I tried to stop him, but he smurfed a snowball right into my smurf and got away!

Did you see who it was?

IT'S A MONSTER!

It's this big! It has enormous teeth, smurfily ugly eyes, and it always smurfs "GRRR" like a monster!

Oh!

Come, come! What are you smurfing us, Greedy Smurf?

It's true, Papa Smurf! It's the same one I smurfed during the picking in the forest! It smurfed us back here!

But that's horrible! We absolutely must smurf something!

Hmm! Whatever the case, we can't let this "thing" smurf our food supply!

So, here's what we'll smurf tomorrow at nightfall! First, Handy Smurf, you smurf a smurf that you'll smurf in the supply room, then we won't smurf at all until something smurfs.

© Peyo 17

21

The next day, as dusk approaches, everything is calm in the village...

Too calm, perhaps...

Good smurf, Handy Smurf!

You, too, Hefty Smurf! Have sweet smurfs!

That night...

CREEE

BING CLAC BOOM

DING DING DING

Ahaa! I knew that would smurf!

Well done, Papa Smurf! Your plan smurfed marvelously!

We'll finally know what it is!

18

OOOH!

GRRRR!

It's a Smurf... Like one of us!

What?!... That's not a monster!

Oh, my!

HOK HOK GRRR!

Is that you again, Jokey Smurf! This time, you're not making anybody laugh with your sillismurf!

Uh, no! Sorry, but this time I have nothing to smurf with this joke! Too bad, too! I hee hee hee!

But who is he then?

?

CHOMP! OWWWWWW!

GRRR!

That Smurf is wild!

That's right, Papa Smurf! If it isn't Jokey Smurf or one of us, who is it?

Well, frankly, Smurfette, I know absosmurfy nothing about it!

So who is this Smurf of whose existence even Papa Smurf seems unaware? And where did he come from?

19

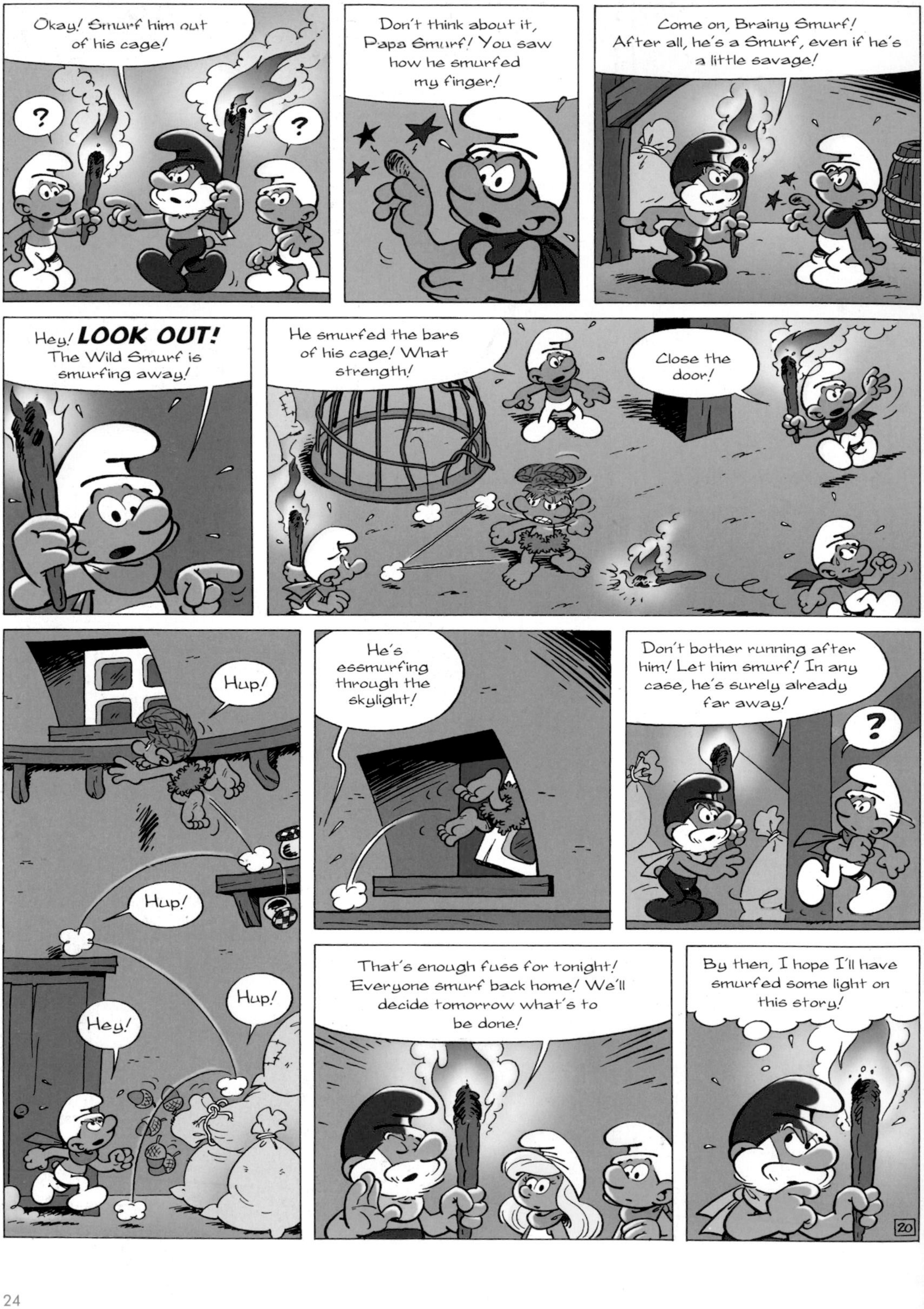
Okay! Smurf him out of his cage!
?
?
Don't think about it, Papa Smurf! You saw how he smurfed my finger!
Come on, Brainy Smurf! After all, he's a Smurf, even if he's a little savage!
Hey! **LOOK OUT!** The Wild Smurf is smurfing away!
He smurfed the bars of his cage! What strength!
Close the door!
Hup!
Hup!
Hey!
Hup!
He's essmurfing through the skylight!
Don't bother running after him! Let him smurf! In any case, he's surely already far away!
?
That's enough fuss for tonight! Everyone smurf back home! We'll decide tomorrow what's to be done!
By then, I hope I'll have smurfed some light on this story!
20

Shortly afterward, in Papa Smurf's laboratory...

"*The Great Book of the Smurfs*" It's been a very long time since I've had occasion to consult it!

For centuries and centuries, the entire history of the Smurfs has been smurfed in here! There must surely be some clue, some kind of hint!

Oh? There! Yes, yes, I remember!

It was a very, very long time ago, on a night when the moon was blue...

Suddenly...

KRAAAK

WAAAH!

And the precious package disappeared into the forest...

The whole night, as well as the following days, we searched the forest tirelessly...

Alas, we soon had to accept the unacceptable, the baby was lost...

After so many years, it's smurfily incredible! Wait til the Smurfs hear of this!

Indeed, the news doesn't leave the Smurfs indifferent...

And that's the whole story!

It's so wonderful!

But then, he's a Smurf like us!

Wow!

That smurfs my mind!

A "Smurf like us," is hasty talk! I've never smurfed someone's finger so savagely, and--

But the poor Smurf! He's going to smurf from cold and hunger in the forest! And he must feel all alone! We can't let him smurf like that!

POW

You're right, Smurfette! I must bring him back to the village and resmurf to him his place among us!

For that, I must gain his trust! You, you, and you, smurf with me! We're going to search for him in the forest!

Shortly after...

How do you think he managed to smurf on his own in the forest, Papa Smurf?

You think he lives in the trees?

I don't smurf at all, but I do hope to find out!

YOOHOO! Wild Smurf! Where are you?

Why did Papa Smurf choose me? I'm sure that savage will bite my finger again!

CRAC

Did you hear that? Something smurfed! There! Behind that tree! I'm... I'm sure it's him!

22

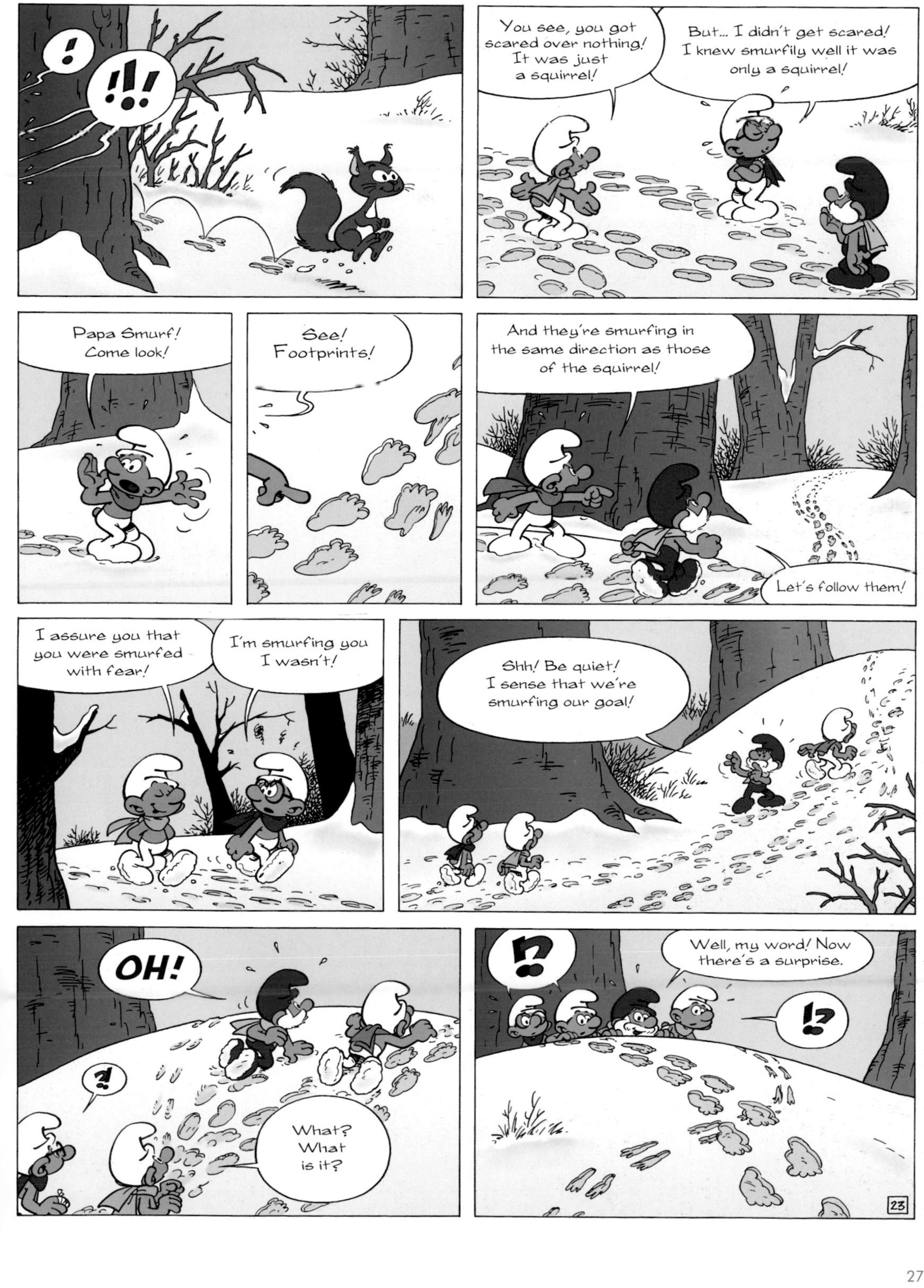
!
!!!
You see, you got scared over nothing! It was just a squirrel!
But... I didn't get scared! I knew smurfily well it was only a squirrel!
Papa Smurf! Come look!
See! Footprints!
And they're smurfing in the same direction as those of the squirrel!
Let's follow them!
I assure you that you were smurfed with fear!
I'm smurfing you I wasn't!
Shh! Be quiet! I sense that we're smurfing our goal!
OH!
?!
What? What is it?
!?
Well, my word! Now there's a surprise.
!?
23

Did you see, Papa Smurf? He's living with squirrels! It's smurfily incredible!

?

SNIF SNIF

The squirrels must have taken him in when he was a babe! That's how he managed to smurf all these years in the forest without dying of hunger!

Uh... Papa Smurf! Look!

GRRRR...

?!

?!

HOK! HOK! HOK!

24

Let's not stay here! He's smurfed our presence!

Oww!

This time it's over! I'm smurfed!

GRRR!

?!

WAP

HA! HA! HA!

?!?!...?

Suddenly, the Wild Smurf's attention is attracted by a cry of distress...

?

Indeed, in its rush to flee, a squirrel fell into the river's icy water...

KUKUKUKUK

Inexorably, it's being carried away by the current...

Without the slightest hesitation, the Wild Smurf hurries to its rescue...

HOK! HOK!

25

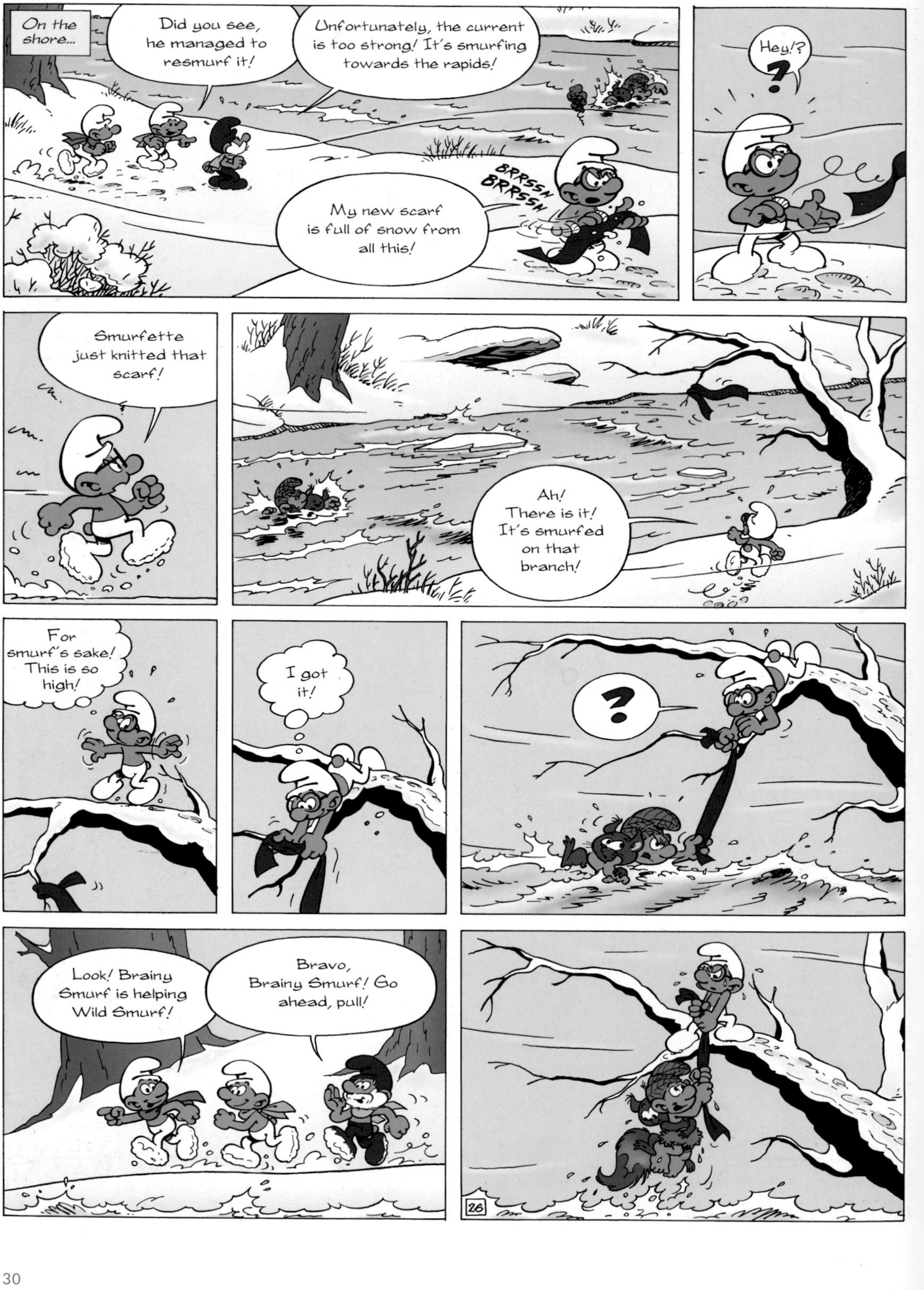
On the shore...
Did you see, he managed to resmurf it!
Unfortunately, the current is too strong! It's smurfing towards the rapids!
BRRSSH BRRSSH
My new scarf is full of snow from all this!
Hey!?
?
Smurfette just knitted that scarf!
Ah! There is it! It's smurfed on that branch!
For smurf's sake! This is so high!
I got it!
?
Look! Brainy Smurf is helping Wild Smurf!
Bravo, Brainy Smurf! Go ahead, pull!
26

> ⸸Grmmbll!⸷ A brand new scarf!

> We saw it all, Brainy Smurf! You smurfed them from drowning!

> I'm a hero!

> Careful, there's the Wild Smurf! Let's observe his reaction!

> HOK! HOK!

> ?

> Now that we've gained his trust, maybe we can convince him to smurf to the village with us!

> Uh... Wild Smurf! If you'd like to smurf to our village! We could smurf you and your squirrels all winter long!

> There! Lots to eat! You smurf there with us?

> !

> HOK! HOK! Yum! Yum!

> That's it! I think he undersmurfed!

> And the Smurfs return to their village accompanied by a strange escort...

Their arrival at the village doesn't go unnoticed...

There they are! They're back!

The Wild Smurf is with them!

I'm the one who smurfed him! I'm a hero!

Where did you smurf him?

He's so funny!

Where is he? Where is he?

Did you see? He's smurfed some leaves to smurf himself a cap! Ha! Ha!

All right, gently! You can see you're scaring him!

He must surely be smurfing from hunger! Yum yum, Wild Smurf?

HOK! HOK! Yum! Yum!

What's more, this expedition has made all five of us hungry! Have a meal made for us! And don't forget to smurf some hazelnuts to the squirrels!

And later...

You'll love my cooking, Wild Smurf!

28

You'll see, I smurfed some little onions in especially for you!

SNIF SNIF

I smurfed you one of my specialties! A smurf supreme with chestnuts and spiced with--

HOK! HOK!

!

YUM

SLURP

GULP

SLURP! YUM! YUM!

Oh!

BURP!

SCRTCH SCRTCH

HA! HA! HA! HA!

HA! HA! HA! HA!

?

WHA! HA! HA!

It seems to me our friend the Wild Smurf will need to smurf a few rules of manners to be able to live among us!...

?

What's more, with your permission, Papa Smurf, I volunteer to smurf him the ABCs of rules of conduct!

Perfect, Brainy Smurf!

29

And that's how the Wild Smurf's education began...

We'll start off by asking Tailor Smurf to smurf you a new outfit, because this one is indecent!

No problem, Brainy Smurf! I have exactly what he needs!

?

I've just smurfed a new line of clothing on which I'm smurfing the final touches! You'll see!

!

And there! What do you smurf of that?

HOK! HOK! HOK!

GRRR!

SCRTCH
SCRTCH
SCRTCH
SCRTCH

SCRTCH...
SCRTCH

!

POOF
BONG

BUNG

CRAK

CLANG

!

I'm not certain it's really what he needs!

Hmmm! In fact, I should leave it more roomy under the smurfs, cut back there, loosen the smurf, and redo it a bit.

A few redos later...

HOK! HOK!

Ah! I see the gentleman is happy! Perfect!

30

And the cap? Not really?

GRRR!

Uh... All right! Okay!

Now that you're presentable, we're going to be able to smurf to work!

Oh, he's so cute with his little loincloth! You could at least smurf introductions, Brainy Smurf!

?

?

Uh... Careful, Smurfette! He's still just a savage!

This Wild Smurf seems as nice as can be! And he looks so strong, too!

!

Why don't you both come smurf some tea at my house?

Snif! Snif!

First I must smurf his education before letting him smurf into society!

Too bad, then! Some other time!

And clearly, the task will be harder than I smurfed!

HOK! HOK!

A little later, once his fervor has settled down...

Okay! First, a language lesson! Today, the word "SMURF"!

HOK HOK
SMURF

The word "SMURF" is composed of the letters "S-M-U-R-F."

S-M-U-R-F

As you can easily smurf, the first syllable is...

YUM CRUNCH

?

31

MY CHALK!

CHOMP-CRUNCH

Okay, that's enough! I've smurfed my fill of emotions for today! As Papa Smurf always says: "One job for a smurf is enough."!

GULP GULP

It's late! Let's go to smurf! Follow me!

There's your bed, Wild Smurf! Your bed! Beddy-byes! Among the Smurfs, everyone smurfs in a bed! You just have to smurf like me!

?

Good night! ⋅Pfffff.⋅

? ZZZZZZZZ

ZZZZZZZ₂

!

In the morning...

Hello, Brainy Smurf! How's it smurfing with our new boarder?

Besides snoring even louder than Lazy Smurf, it's smurfing!

Because I'd like to smurf to his education, too!

You, Jokey Smurf?

I have a gift for him! Here, Wild Smurf, it's for you!

?

Go on, you can open it! It's a surprise! Hee hee hee!

?

32

Hey! No! Not like...

...that!

KABLAM

?

! !

Hee hee hee! I never thought of smurfing that gag like that! I think we'll get along!

WHA HA HA HA! KABLAM!

Throughout the winter, Brainy Smurf is busy teaching him the basics of life in society...

?

And if sometimes the results aren't as expected...

Brainy Smurf never gets discouraged...

?

But one day...

HOK HOK CRNMF CHRUMF SMURF

Well, Brainy Smurf, how is the Wild Smurf's education smurfing?

⁙Boohoohoo!⁙ I'll never make it, Papa Smurf! It's a catasmurfre!

Come, come!

Catasmurfre!

?

Did you hear, Papa Smurf? The word "smurf"! He smurfed it! Go ahead, Wild Smurf! Repeat again: "smurf"!

SMURF

33

37

Smurf!

After that, the Wild Smurf makes rapid progress, arousing the admiration of some...

But also the jealousy of others...

And then, the spring comes...

Come look, everyone! The first buds are here!

Yes! Nature is resmurfing its rights! And since ash makes excellent fertilizer, the plants will grow again very quickly!

YIPPEE! THE FOREST WILL SOON BE LIKE BEFORE!

?

Look, Azrael, spring has returned! And high time, I was almost out of food! The animals will come back and I can lay down traps again!

And since the Smurfs have gone away, this spring is off to a promising start! Heh heh heh!

Later, much later...

Are you going into the forest, Smurfette?

We're going for a smurfnic, Papa Smurf! Nature resmurfing is so beautiful!

34

Your friends, the squirrels! We hadn't smurfed them in a long time!

HOK! HOK! 'Quirrels!

OH! Look!

?

The poor animal! Who could have smurfed that!

I wouldn't be surprised if it were...

CRAG

?!

?

?!

Gargamel! EEEEEEK!

!

SMURFS?! But I thought you'd left the forest!

Run away, Wild Smurf!

GRRR...

And what's more, you're opening my traps! You'll pay for that!

GRRR...

35

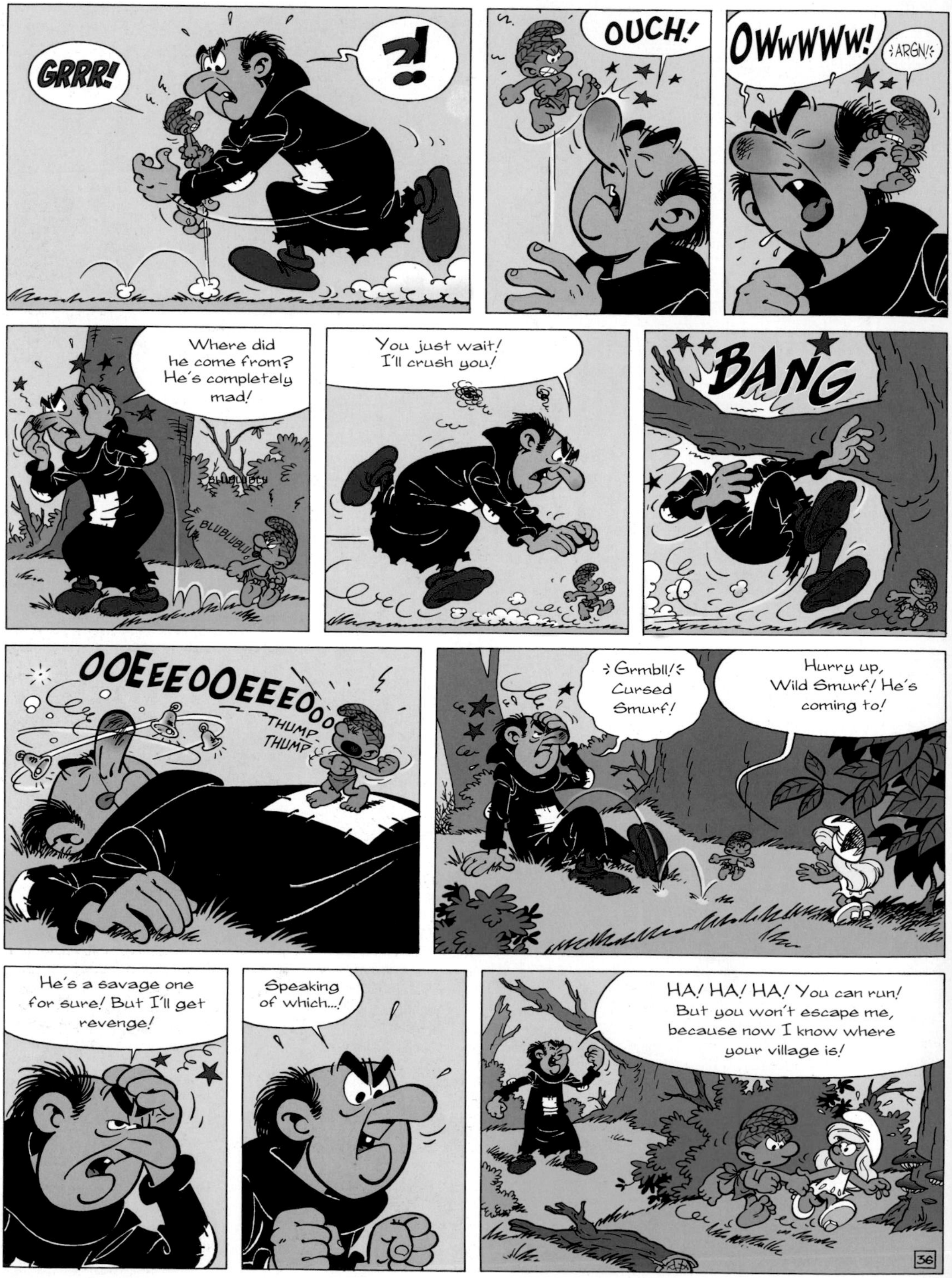
GRRR!
?!
OUCH!
OWWWWW!
ARGN!
Where did he come from? He's completely mad!
BLUBLUBLU
BLUBLUBLU
You just wait! I'll crush you!
BANG
OOEEEEOOEEEEOOO
THUMP THUMP
Grmbl! Cursed Smurf!
Hurry up, Wild Smurf! He's coming to!
He's a savage one for sure! But I'll get revenge!
Speaking of which...!
HA! HA! HA! You can run! But you won't escape me, because now I know where your village is!
36

Papa Smurf! Papa Smurf!

It's Gargamel! Back there, in the forest! He smurfed us, but the Wild Smurf smurfed him! But he said he knew where our village was smurfed!

Gargamel! The footprints! So it was him!

And unfortunately, the forest isn't leafy enough yet to keep him from smurfing the way to the village!

What are we going to do, Papa Smurf? I'm scared!

Something's coming! It's him!

Everyone, smurf! Go hide in the forest!

Ahaaaa! I see their village!

Surrender, you blasted Smurfs! You're doomed! You can no longer escape me!

Well?! Where did they all go?

37

Something moved in the bushes!

CRAC!

Shh!

?!

Curses! They've hidden in the forest!

You can go on hiding! One day you'll have to return to your village!

And now that nothing can keep me from finding the path again, I can come back whenever I like!

So, see you tomorrow! Or maybe right away, who knows? Heh heh heh!

It's terrible, Papa Smurf! What are we going to smurf?

In any case, there's no question of resmurfing to the village, it's too dangerous!

Hok! Hok! Smurfs live in forest! With 'quirrels! Gar'mel never find!

?

Wild Smurf show!

38

Clothes no good! Smurf leaves!

?

A few moments later...

Hok! Hok! 'derful!

I don't know if I was right to trust Jokey Smurf to smurf my camouflage!

SCRTCH SCRTCH

I find this smurfily exotic! It's too bad I don't have my make-up case!

Perfect! Now let's see to smurfing ourselves some shelter for the night!

The next day, the Smurfs get organized...

Look out! Everyone smurf! Gargamel's returning to the village!

This time, I'll catch them by surprise!

AHAAAA! I got you!

39

‡ Grmbl! ‡ They still haven't returned to their village!

But I'll get them! On my word as a sorcerer!

Hee hee hee! Old Gargamel! He's so stupid!

And the days pass...

Look out! He's back!

Identically...

Guess who's coming to smurf?

Monotonously...

Hey, guys, it's time! Here he is!

Almost tiringly...

♪

Until the day when...

I have to come up with something else! I'm going mad! For once I can find the way back to their village!

‡ Pff! ‡ This has gotten boring! I'm going to smurf a little joke on him!

?

♭

BOP

HEE! HEE! HEE! HEE! HOK! HEE! HEE! HEE! HEE! HEE! HEE! HEE! HEE! HEE! HEE! HEE! HEE! HEE! HEE! HEE!

?!?

Cursed Smurfs! They're mocking me! But how come I can't see them?

Hmm! It wouldn't surprise me if they camouflaged themselves and are living in the forest!

Well, I have a surprise of my own for them!

40

And later...

No longer having to smurf to the dam, no longer having to take care of the house! I love smurfing in the forest after all!

Remember that the smurf makes work for idle hands! And also, don't forget that Gargamel is still lurking about and that forewarned is foresmurfed!

?

Well said, runt!

HA! HA! HA! You see, you're not the only ones who can camouflage yourselves!

Smurf me! Help!

There's no use bawling! Nobody will come to your rescue!

?

ARGN!

OWWWWWW!

BROMP

Go ahead, Wild Smurf! Smurf him a lesson!

GRRRR...

You again, you rabid smurf!

This time your goose is cooked!

BLUBLUBLU

41

45

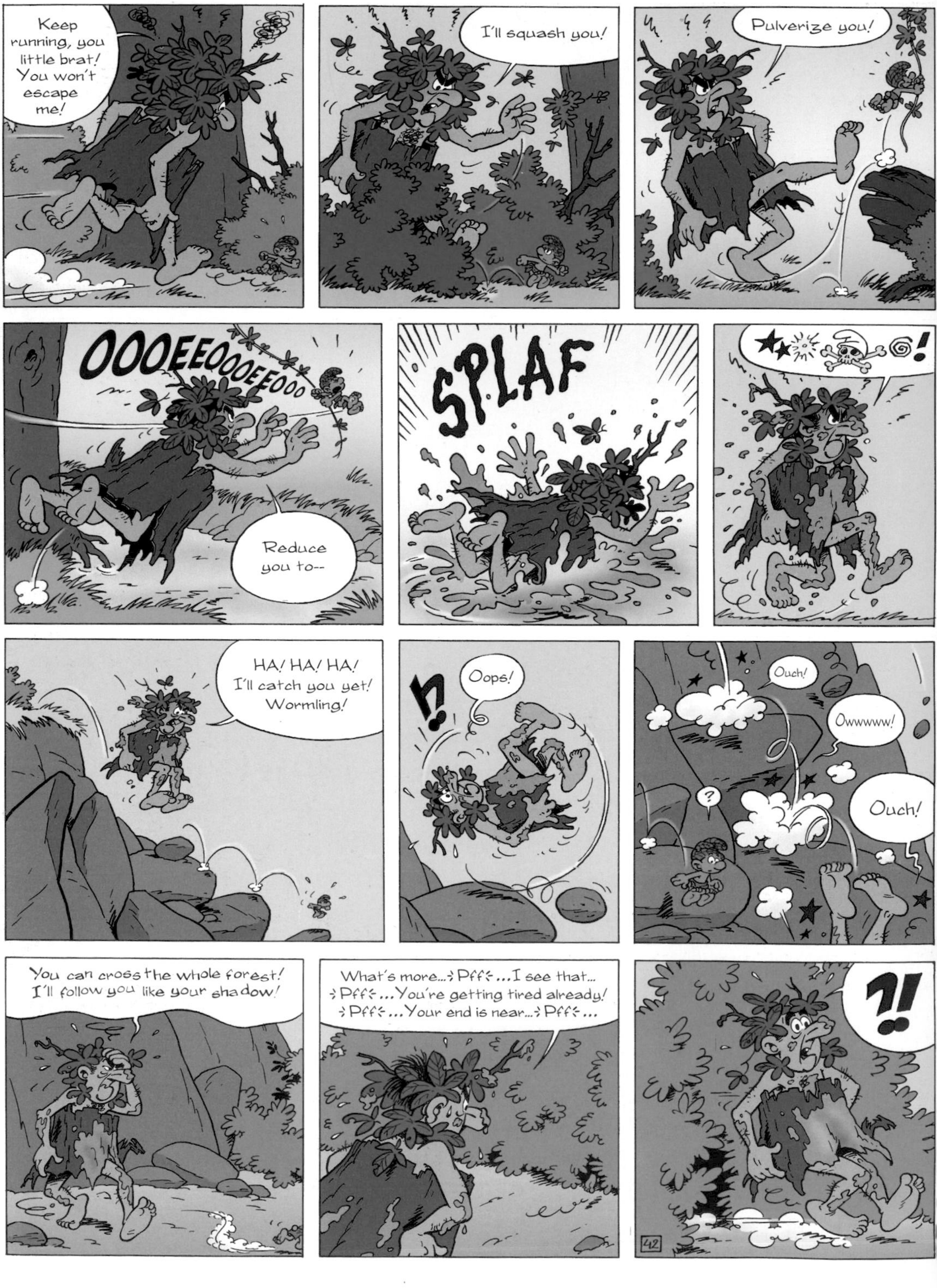

Keep running, you little brat! You won't escape me!
I'll squash you!
Pulverize you!
OOOEEOOOEEOOo
Reduce you to--
SPLAF
HA! HA! HA! I'll catch you yet! Wormling!
Oops!
Ouch!
Owwwww!
?
Ouch!
You can cross the whole forest! I'll follow you like your shadow!
What's more... Pff... I see that... Pff... You're getting tired already! Pff... Your end is near... Pff...
?!
42

Who is that maniac? Seize him!

But... Oh, come on! Let me go!

Silence, or I'll knock you out! You'll explain yourself to the bailiff!

Hee hee hee! Poor Gargamel! He's smurfed himself into a fine mess!

By the time he gets out, the forest will have regrown, and he won't smurf his way back to the village again! Let's go home!

TOK TOK

I assure you, Milord! They're little blue goblins with white caps! They're all over the forest! They're making my life impossible!

I have important things to do! Send this maniac to the madhouse!

In the forest, the Smurfs make their way back to their village...

And the guards knocked him out and then smurfed him almost naked to the humans' village!

HA! HA! HA! HA! HA!

43

47

Well, Wild Smurf, you're not smurfing back with us?

Not smurf back to village! Stay in forest with 'quirrels!

I understand! Life in the village is, no doubt, not right for you, but don't ever forget that you can come smurf us a little visit whenever you like...

Dry your tears, Smurfette! It's surely better this way!

⸎Boohoo!⸎

Hok, Hok!

TOM TOM

You see, we mustn't always try to change others, at any cost, to smurf like us!

But... He must get bored all alone in the forest!

Many months later...

⸎RHAA!⸎ This blasted forest has grown back! I'll never find the way to that cursed village! I'll get revenge! I'll get revenge! I'll get revenge! I'll get revenge! I'll...

END

SCHOOL FOR FAIRIES

Baby Smurf has the measles! Smurfette won't be able to smurf school!

Awesome!

So, no school for us?

YIPPEE!

Today, Smurflings, you'll smurf to the fairy school! Lady Severe will smurf you there to her class!

We're not fairies!

LINE UP AND BE QUIET!

A bit later...

¿Pff!¿ Is the school far away still?

Very, very far! Sing to give yourself some energy! One... Two...

♪ Another mile to smurf, ♫ ♯ to smurf, to smurf, to smurf... ♪

Sing a little louder! I'm a little deaf!

ANOTHER MILE TO SMURF, TO SMURF, TO SMURF, YOU LITTLE SMURFS!

?

Here's our pretty castle!

SMURFLINGS! And they're heading right towards the fairy school! Heh heh!

Look-- Watchdogs!

They look fierce!

They must be, for there are wolves in the woods!

WOOF WOOF WOOF

School

?

Maybe I'll have a chance to capture them before they go into the school.

© Peyo 1

YEOOWWW!

It's a wolf trap!

OOOOWW! OOOOOWW! OWW-OWW!

WOLVES!

I'm scared!

Go, watchdogs! WOLVES! Go get 'em!

WOOF WOOF WOOF

HELP! WATCHDOGS! OOOOOOOWWW!

WOOF WOOF WOOF

These are the fairy school students! I hope you all get along! I'm very strict about discipline! Follow me!

Hi, I'm Sassette!

Hey, Nat, Slouchy.. There's nothing but girls here!

SILENCE! Today, a lesson on magical energy! Who can tell me what this is called?

Me!

It's a magic wand, teacher!

Teacher's pet!

Very good! Can you read this sentence now?

ABRACADABRA

Uh... Abra... Cadabra!

Give us a little demonstration now!

ABRACADABRA... ZOOO!

ABRA DABRA

Pff!

That's easy! I can smurf that, myself!

Okay, Snappy! You show us!

Conjugate the verbe: "to smurf"!

I smurf ...ous

© Peyo

50

DING DONG DING

It's time to eat! No running down to the dining hall! Let's go!

?

YIPPEE!

Yum yum!

smurf smur smurf smurf smu am

Leeks! Yuck!

You'll eat your soup or I'll make you swallow the whole pot!

That's nasty! I don't want any!

?

It's time to go to bed! Follow me in two rows!

What?! Smurfing to bed so early? That smurfs!

You'll sleep in the fairy dormitory!

Goodnight, ma'am!

⹁Whew⹁ What a day! I'm so tired!

ZZ!

I should find someone to help me! I'm too old to take care of everything by myself...

Hey, wake up! The teacher is snoring. Let's go smurf the fairies, disguised as ghosts!

Hee hee! Good idea!

zZZz...

Shhh!

Hee hee hee!

EEEEEEEEEEE

?

3

© Peyo

51

OOoBOOOOoBOOOOO! EEEE! EEEEE!

What's going on in here?!

It's them, ma'am! They came in here smurfed as ghosts!

EEEE! EEEEE!

HEE HEE! HEE!

I'm warning you, if you don't leave the girls alone, I'll tell Papa Smurf!

It wasn't us!

ZZ!

Those Smurflings are maddening!

The next morning...

How can I get myself into that castle?

The school is looking for a monitor! Hoho! That's just what I needed! Now I just have to drink my magic potion that makes me tiny! Heh heh heh!

A little later...

Uh... I'm here about the announcement. Um...

Come in. I'll introduce you!

I have to go away, but I've found a class monitor for you! You all behave!

Hello, teacher!

Um.. Hello!

That old fogey looks weird!

?

Be firm with the Smurflings, because they're scamps!

I can handle them, have no fear! Heh heh! Bon voyage!

?

4 © Peyo

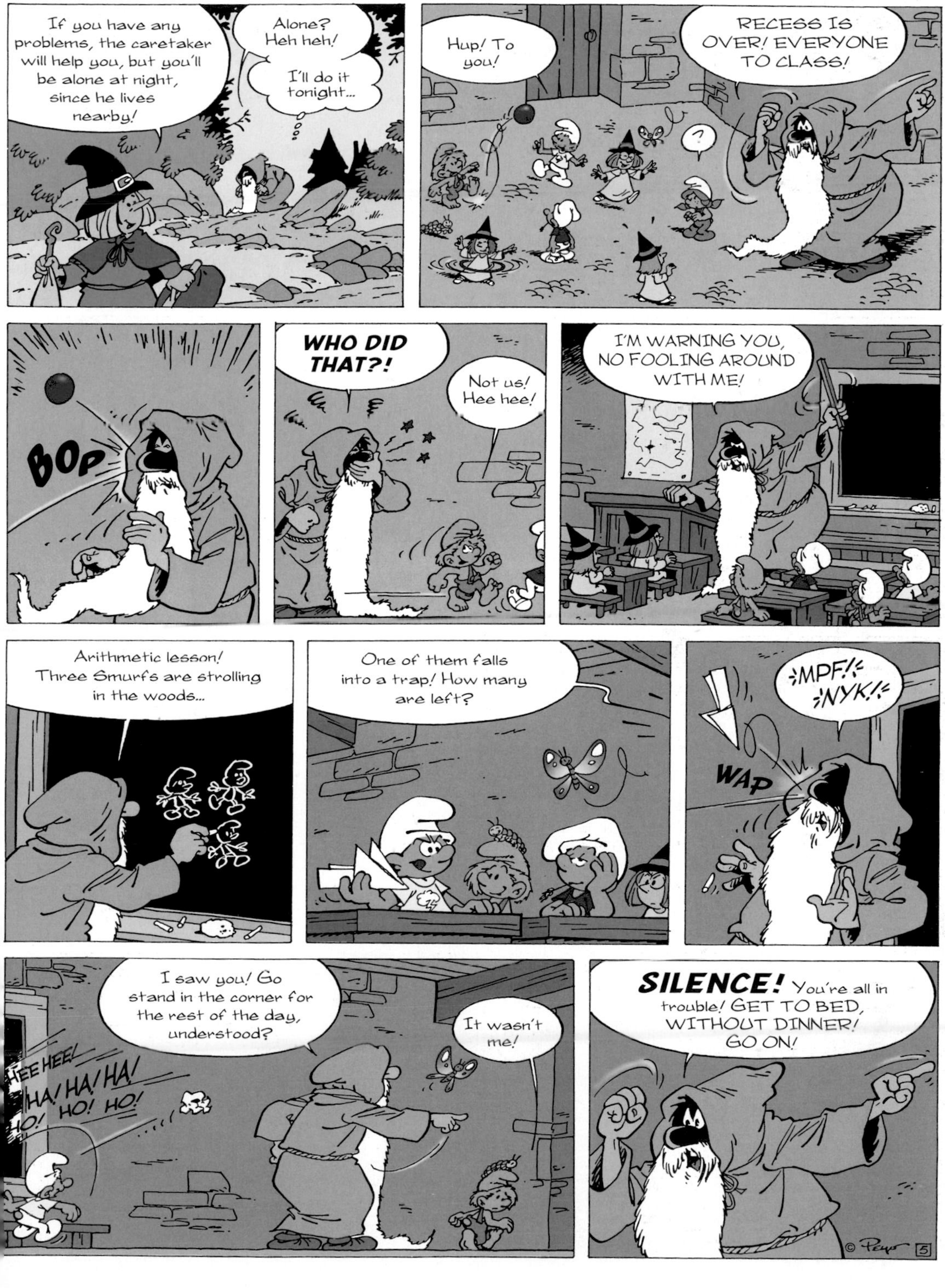
If you have any problems, the caretaker will help you, but you'll be alone at night, since he lives nearby!
Alone? Heh heh!
I'll do it tonight...
Hup! To you!
RECESS IS OVER! EVERYONE TO CLASS!
BOP
WHO DID THAT?!
Not us! Hee hee!
I'M WARNING YOU, NO FOOLING AROUND WITH ME!
Arithmetic lesson! Three Smurfs are strolling in the woods...
One of them falls into a trap! How many are left?
MPF! NYK!
WAP
I saw you! Go stand in the corner for the rest of the day, understood?
It wasn't me!
HEE HEE! HA! HA! HA! HO! HO! HO!
SILENCE! You're all in trouble! GET TO BED, WITHOUT DINNER! GO ON!
© Peyo 5

He forgot about us, Butterfly!

DON'T LOOK BACK! GET TO YOUR ROOM!

Old fogey!

OOPS! I stepped on my beard!

Oh! He's smurfed over his beard!

BAM

♪ GRMBLL! ♪ Quick, let me adjust this fake beard!

GARGAMEL! THAT'S GARGAMEL!

Uh oh! What do we do? He's going to wait till night and smurf my friends!

I have an idea, Butterfly! You'll smurf this message to Papa Smurf!

Smurf quickly to the Smurf Village, Butterfly. I'll warn the others!

Everyone into your rooms and sleep, or else, LOOK OUT!

He's not very nice!

I'll wait till midnight to capture them all! I have time for a little nap!

© Peyo

ZZZZ...

Shh! It's me! No noise! The monitor is Gargamel! Let's smurf out of here fast!

?! GARGAMEL?!

Come on, let's warn the girls!

SHH!

ZZZ...

GARGAMEL?! Are you sure?

Yes, he smurfed on a fake beard! We have to hurry!

?

It's high!

SHH!

I'm scared!

At that moment...

By the devil! Dummies! They fooled me! Where are they?

There they are! ⸗RHAAAAA!⸗ They're going to get away!

I still have a chance to catch them down below!

Well?

The sheets are too short! I'm afraid to smurf!

?

Don't worry... I'll catch you! HA! HA! HA! HA!

© Peyo

I wouldn't smurf that if I were you, Gargamel!

It's Butterfly with Papa Smurf! HURRAY!

Huh? I'll capture you, too! HA! HA! HA!

I'm not alone, see!

THE WATCHDOGS!

WOOF WOOF

WOOF WOOF WOOF

HELP! HELP!

Butterfly is a good messenger. I was able to alert the caretaker!

The next morning...

It's all my fault! I shouldn't have left to go fetch my sister!

Don't you worry, Lady Severe! Baby Smurf is better, so Smurfette will teach their class in the village!

I can't let you leave without inviting you to the school party!

Say yes, Papa Smurf!

Later...

I'm glad this is all ending happily!

Thanks, Lady Severe!

Tralalalalii LALALAAA DZEEM BOOM PWHAT TOOROO FLOOT

Meanwhile...

WOOF WOOF WOOF

OH, NO! I'm out of the antidote to return to my normal size! NOOOOOO!

© Peyo

8 END

WATCH OUT FOR PAPERCUTZ™

Welcome to the teeth-gnashing, tree-swinging, twenty-first SMURFS graphic novel from Papercutz, that Wild Bunch dedicated to publishing great graphic novels for all ages. I'm Jim Salicrup, your wild 'n' crazy Smurf-in-Chief, here to celebrate reaching our 21st SMURFS graphic novel. (Hey, there wasn't any room to celebrate in our 20th graphic novel, so we added more pages to the series, and we'll celebrate our 21st instead!)

Since Papercutz was founded over ten years ago, by publisher Terry Nantier and me, we've always wanted to publish the very best comics for all ages. And since 2010, when we first published THE SMURFS #1 "The Purple Smurfs," we've been proud to publish Peyo's wonderful comics. Not only have we been publishing THE SMURFS, but we've also published…

THE SMURFS ANTHOLOGY – Re-presenting the Smurfs stories in the order they were originally published and at the same size they were originally published. Also featuring Peyo's *Johan and Peewit* (the court page and jester) comics that introduced the Smurfs, and insightful commentary by Matt. Murray, Smurfologist.

THE SMURFS AND FRIENDS – Presenting Smurfs comics and The Smurfs comic strips, as well as *Johan and Peewit* comics that don't include our little blue buddies, also Peyo's *Benny Breakiron* (the super-strong French boy) comics, and more behind-the-scenes historical essays by Matt. Murray.

And coming soon, Peyo's **PUSSYCAT**, a one-volume, complete-as-possible collection of Pussycat cartoons and comic strips featuring an irrepressible cat that endlessly gets into funny situations. (Maybe we should change our name to PaperCATz, if we're publishing this…?) To give you an example of exactly what I'm talking about, enjoy the special preview of PUSSYCAT on the following pages.

So, here we are—the twenty-first North American volume of THE SMURFS! I want to personally thank Joe Johnson (Smurflator), Adam Grano (Smurfic Designer), Janice Chiang (Lettering Smurfette), and Matt. Murray (Smurf Consultant), for their smurftastic work on each and every one of those twenty-one SMURFS graphic novels! We've been a great team, and I look forward to keep on working with all of you! But most of all, I want to thank you for supporting this series and Papercutz, and hope that you continue to enjoy the great comics created by Peyo yet to come from Papercutz!

Smurf you later,
Thanks,

Jim

STAY IN TOUCH!
EMAIL: salicrup@papercutz.com
WEB: papercutz.com
TWITTER: @papercutzgn
FACEBOOK: PAPERCUTZGRAPHICNOVELS
SMURF MAIL: Papercutz, 160 Broadway, Suite 700, East Wing, New York, NY 10038

Well, well!

Pussycat! Do you know what you are?...

?

You're of a digitigrade, carnivorous, mammalian species!... Oh, yes!

!

But-- But, Pussycat, it's not an insult! It's the definition from the dictionary!

Gag #184 appeared in *Spirou* #1671 of April 23, 1970.
It was later republished in album 2, page 21, in January 1977.

PUSSYCAT BY Peyo   MADE IN JAPAN

Gag #190 appeared in album 1, page 12, in October 1977

PUSSYCAT BY Peyo   THE TONIC

Gag #192 appeared in *Spirou* #1439 of November 11, 1965.
It was later republished in album 1, page 15, in January 1976.

Gag #193 appeared in *Spirou* #1469 of June 9, 1966.
It was later republished in album 2, page 12, in January 1977.

 **PUSSYCAT** FISHING PROHIBITED

Gag #196 appeared in *Spirou* #1545 of November 23, 1967.
It was later republished in album 1, page 27, in January 1976.

Gag #200 appeared in *Spirou* #1639 of September 11, 1969.
It was later republished in album 1, page 33, in January 1976.

 PUSSYCAT BY *Peyo* LANGUAGE CLASSES

Gag #204 appeared in *Spirou* #1479 of August 18, 1966.
It was later republished in album 1, page 19, in January 1976.

Gag #210 appeared in album 3, page 35, in October 1977.

PUSSYCAT BY Peyo — AERIAL PURSUIT

Gag #212 appeared in *Spirou* #1456 of March 10, 1966.
It was later republished in album 1, page 45, in January 1976.

PUSSYCAT BY *Peyo*

INNOCENT GAMES

Gag #214 appeared in *Spirou* #1488 of October 20, 1966.
It was later republished in album 2, page 20, in January 1977.

PUSSYCAT BY *Peyo*

THE BILL-POSTER

Gag #216 appeared in *Spirou* #1489 of October 27, 1966.
It was later republished in album 3, page 34, in October 1977.

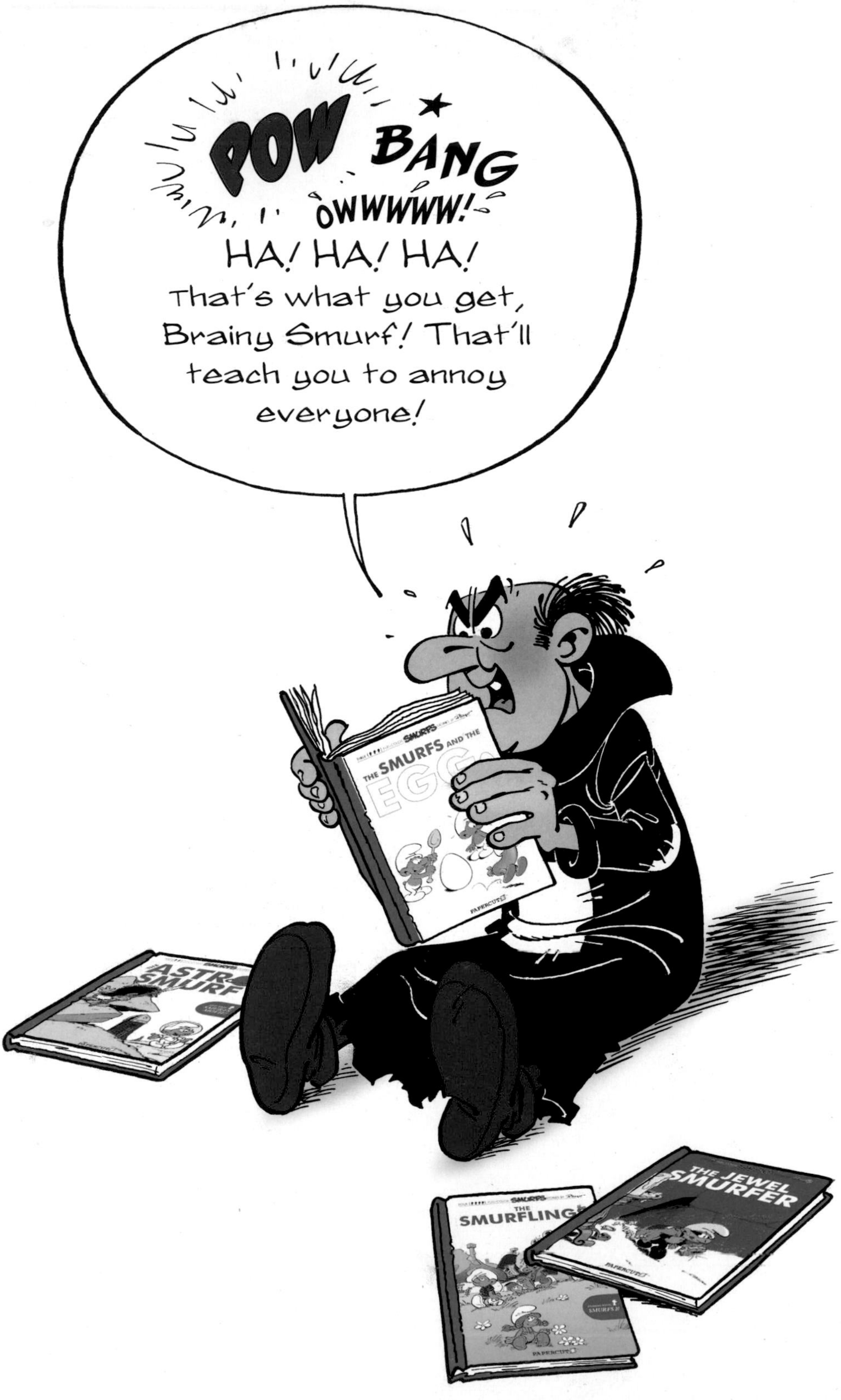
POW BANG
OWWWWW!
HA! HA! HA!
That's what you get, Braainy Smurf! That'll teach you to annoy everyone!
THE SMURFS AND THE EGG
ASTRO SMURF
THE SMURFLINGS
THE JEWEL SMURFER